Wish Upon a Space Station

ABIGAIL JENNIFER TOWNSON

Copyright © 2024 by Abigail Jennifer Townson

All rights reserved.

No part of this book may be reproduced in any form or by any electronic or mechanical means, including information storage and retrieval systems, without written permission from the author, except for the use of brief quotations in a book review.

Author's Note

This book is inspired by my late Uncle, Paul Cunliffe who sadly lost his life way too soon in 2008.

He always got me and my family to look out for the space station going by at night and now whenever we see it go by, we like to think he is up there circulating around the world looking after us too.

I'd like to dedicate this book to him and my family who inspire and support me to grow each day with the love and compassion for my career and life choices.

Chapter 1

DREAMING AND BELIEVING

I snore, I fidget, I scratch good sunglasses, I pee roughly every 20 minutes due to the fact I have the bladder of about a 2-year-old child because I have endometriosis which also causes extreme bloat, bad period pain, gut issues, and the rest! Oh, and my knees are fucked. It's a fun time daily. I move things around a lot because I get bored and change my mind about a million times a day, but I think I only do that because I'm not in control of my life right now - Oh, and my sinuses are completely screwed too so I have to use a natural rinsing solution every morning-what a beautiful sight and sound to wake up to hey! Honestly so much of a turn on, right!? HOWEVER, I figured that maybe if I just put it all out there and my future person can decide for himself if he can deal with it if he knows it all right away. Like a bare all story hey.

I'm 36 years old and recently, I've come to the realisation that I've only ever had one piss poor relationship. If you can even call it a relationship - it only lasted 3 months. Just some guy from college that I thought I was in love with and who I thought loved me back...I think I was like 19 or 20 at the time...that's late for most girls I know, but the thing is, I'm not most girls, nor do I want to be. I say one relationship, I've had other "things" since him but that first one was the one I got so sucked into! That's late for most girls I know, but the thing is, I'm not most girls, nor do I want to be. I finally love who I am! That age didn't bother me because we all have a different timeline, and it was when I felt ready to trust someone...

Why do I always put men on some kind of pedestal like they are so fucking amazing. I need to protect my heart and they need to know how good I am for once. I must stop pretending that I already know who the person is that I want to see in my future. I haven't met him yet and that's OK. I just want that different kind of love, the kind of love that they make you feel is possible in the movies. Well, if you believe it enough, it really can come true and it's what happens when you wish upon a space station. Let me take you back to my summer of 2019.... Pre-World Pandemic and all that!!....

It was an interesting summer to say the least and I never imagined that a life I only ever dreamt of would become so very real!

I just needed a change, I needed to get away. Something I had come to terms with was, that the only thing I'm not scared of committing to is to love and being loved by someone special but then again when someone is into me, I get so scared of rejection or losing myself in someone. I still need to be me first and foremost.

This feeling that often creeps in of not being good enough for someone to love goes back to my teenage years. I was never the popular girl, nor did I want to be. I didn't walk around with my skirt up to my panties nor did I want to.

I was never the one to get the kiss from the guy I liked or even get asked to the school dance. Nor would I have even cared about a stupid dance, but it would have been just a little bit awesome to feel a little bit special.

It's hard when you feel like your best friend might end up with the guy you've got a crush on because you think she's more pretty than you are or maybe she's more experienced than you or her abs are tighter than yours!

Growing up, I never felt cool enough in school, or good looking enough for the lads or thin enough-all the things I thought a guy wanted in a girl and I guess it held me back in believing I would ever find real love, the kind of love that you see in the movies. The kind of love where he won't care about any imperfections, because he'll love you for you - maybe even the things you don't love about yourself. But if you think that all guys are the same, you'll never let yourself trust the right one and by right one, I mean the right one for you. I would doubt my own self-worth and for what!!? They didn't like you, so what! Next, move on, someone else will appreciate you one day. I say that, but it really is not so simple is it.

I always believed I wasn't worthy of love. At the end of the day, it wasn't me, it was them and the fact that my stars hadn't aligned yet with the right person. Rejection after rejection - The guy in high-school always went for the other girl in the room. The guy in college always ends up taking the other girl home at the party and I'm left there reeling from the effects of rejection and feeling like I'll never be loved while some other girl gets to enjoy attention and affection and I'm there chasing a fairy tale ending that some guy is just going to come right up to me and ask me out or better still, actually be interested in the chase and be bold enough to take a chance. It does start to have a negative effect on you if it happens all the time. You do start to wonder if it really is you. You try so hard but really it shouldn't be this hard. I felt all these things until I met Ben. Ben was different, or so I hoped he would be.

I had been spending a lot of time soul searching for myself and I've always been a firm believer in that everything happens for a reason, but it wasn't until I looked up at the clear London sky one night, watching the space station go by that I felt a shift in my world, like I could make my dreams come true.

I'm a big manifester you see. You must imagine yourself already in the world you want to be in, for it to become a reality. Have you ever wished upon a space station, wished for something greater than you ever believed in? I used to think that leaving it up to fate or the universe was something to be laughed at... But the truth is, the universe will send what you attract and what you truly put in. I am worthy of love, of any kind of love - it's just that I haven't come across anyone special enough to be worthy of mine yet and I've got a whole lot to give back if someone would just take a chance.

Anyway, back to the whole space station thing and my inspiration behind it. My late uncle always showed me and my family when the space station would be going by in the night's sky, and it always makes me think of him now. It gives me a sense of hope and makes me feel like there's something so special happening up there and it really does make you feel magic is happening to believe that things can and will change if you want that change bad enough.

The next day, I decided enough was enough, so I decided to pack in my soul-sucking full-time job as a real estate agent in London. I was miserable there. I was practically working to pay the bills and never got to see life for what it's worth.

I just felt like the universe was trying to tell me something and I had to go and grab it. So, I took a summer job back home where I grew up in the Algarve, Portugal at a kid's camp to become one of the performance coaches there. I trained as an actress but like anyone who is an actor knows, you've often got to have regular jobs that actually pay, so this was my chance to get back into acting again."

My besties Donna and Tara were helping me pack up my life in London and we were going through all the memories from college days, nights out in London and all the things we'd experienced from our awesome times together. There was a lot of wine, dancing and nights out in Leicester Square involved over the years. I was sad to be leaving them behind, but it was the perfect farewell to celebrate my new chapter. They were so happy for me, and we knew our friendship would never change because we're that strong- we're the 3 musketeers for god's sake! They are both married and have kids and they're always telling me that I will get that man, that different kind of love that I've always wanted but only when it's someone who knocks me back for six to be worth it cause I'm a catch, or so my girls say! I've got so much love to give.

I just wanted to see and hear the waves at sunrise and sunset as they crashed against the shore; I wanted to feel the sun beaming down on my skin. I wanted that warm, fuzzy feeling that will make me feel like anything is possible and that this is my life, my life-changing moment. I wanted to believe that I was happy on my own first. And it's ok if you don't have your shit together before you meet someone ok girls...I mean, who really has their whole shit together anyway! You can grow, heal together with the right person. I just knew London wasn't that place for me to make that happen anymore. I wanted to be in the moment and gain some more life experience. I want to ride a vespa on the open Italian roads, I wanted to jump into a waterfall and just feel alive and share it with someone.

I guess I was forever holding out hope that maybe,

just maybe, one day someone would want to be seen with me in public and be proud to kiss me and hold my hand and love me just the way I deserve to be loved. That person is never me, but I guess all the rejections were leading me to better people who deserved for me to invest in them.

I told myself that the next guy I met was going to want to move mountains and oceans to want to be with me because he'd take a risk and he won't be afraid, and he'll want to move countries if it means being with me.

All the engagements, all the weddings that follow with all the baby announcements used to all be a bit too much for me when it was never happening for me! It was more than I could handle emotionally. Of course, I'm always massively happy for the family and friends whose lives are moving on, but I couldn't help that heart-breaking feeling that mine never felt like it was and that felt like another reason I needed some space and to get away... but you know what, I picked myself back up like I always do and surrounded myself with the people who matter most. I was ok that I hadn't met him yet because I'm too busy creating the life I want for myself first.

Chapter 2

THE FIRST ENCOUNTER

I don't ask for much in life, just a vision I truly believe in. It's not a complicated one. It's a world that is calm and kind. It's a simple life. I don't ask for things, I only hope for feelings, memories and people to help complete them. I ask for health and happiness. With these good vibes, I know it's possible for anything to happen. It's great to be on your own sometimes. Just to gather your thoughts and feelings. To believe in a world where everything you ever dreamed of comes true. Just put it out to the universe and the universe will give it back to you. Work hard for it and it will and can happen.

The day of my flight to Portugal arrived and I was super confident and happy and nothing was going to get in my way! I opened the front door and stepped into a massive puddle and then some dog shite on the way to the train station so that was a great fun start!

"Ohhhhhhh For fucks saaaakkke!" I screamed out.

I was listening to some upbeat songs as I walked to the train station.... Rain was pouring down; I was getting in a right huff because nothing was going my way. Of course, my fucking umbrella broke, and my shoes and socks became completely soaked and I got wet through and through by the time I got to the train station.

"Calm the fuck down, Haley...I told myself."

I listened to music while I got my ticket and onto the train. When I got onto the train, there was no space anywhere, so I sat on the floor and took a deep breath. As I was writing in my notebook, I kept looking out at the window and all around me for inspiration for my affirmations ...

This is what I wrote:

Dear universe, here I go, I give you my all. Please be kind.

I am a successful performer-I have worked really damn hard to get here.

I write and narrate a lot, mostly animation work.

I am the voice for a lot of commercials.

I perform as an actress in TV and theatre.

I sing in a band part time.

I run my own workshops.

I am currently earning between 50-60 grand a year, sometimes more.

When the train pulled into Gatwick Airport, I got all giddy and excited as I hear the Tannoy say:

"The next station is Gatwick Airport, please take all your personal belongings with you when you leave the

train, mind the gap between the train and platform, this train will terminate here."

When I eventually made it through all the bollox and faff of the massive security queue, I finally sat down in my aisle seat, headphones on, notebook and pen straight back out.

An attractive 30-something Australian (of course he's an Aussie- it's just my thing!) was also on my flight looking around for his seat but damn it, he was right at the front plane aisle with his ticket in his hand looking for his seat. I kept going up to the bathroom just to get a sneaky peak...Good lord, he was so fucking hot- I wouldn't kick him out of bed for farting.

When I sat back down from my sussing out sesh, I began some more manifesting...

I have met the love of my life!

He is Australian- because obviously - that's just my vibe, I always fall for them -ask my mates!

He is gorgeous, kind, warm, loving, generous, sexy but cute with it, he is respectful, funny, the right amount of romantic without being too soppy. He surprises me when I "least expect it".

He loves his family.

He makes me belly laugh.

I fancy the pants off him!

He irritates me sometimes, but this makes our relationship challenging and interesting.

He loves to relax without technology.

He can switch off but is also hard working and driven.

He loves holidays, cold and hot.

We have similar and different tastes in music and films.

He looks after his health and body.

He does not smoke or do drugs.

He drinks on a social level, like me. He knows when to stop and he is not an asshole when he's drunk.

He likes the simplicity of a walk on the beach and spending quality time with each other.

We have our own space too, he does his thing, I do mine.

He loves Christmas, lets me watch crap rom coms.

He loves dogs.

He is also in his 30's and would like to get married one day.

He sees kids in his future.

He has banter, is flirty with me, he keeps things fresh and exciting.

He makes me feel like the most important person in the room and gives me no reason to feel jealous.

He drives.

We have moved in together to a beautiful, start out apartment overlooking the sea.

He is ambitious, creative, knowledgeable, smart, trusting, knows what he wants and gets it.

He's one of the lads, but in a good, funny way.

He is fab at meeting new people; I never need to worry at a dinner party. He could charm anyone.

He believes in me and is very supportive of my freelance career.

He helps with the dishes.

He is the right amount of perfect without being too perfect.

He allows me to be me and allows himself to be himself too.

We see each other's strengths and weaknesses and help each other grow.

We hardly argue, if we do it is only about things and not each other.

He's a great support, is always there for me.

He knows just how to calm me down if I'm upset or stressed.

I looked around me to check if anyone was watching and then out to the stunning night sky from the window. I did my little random ritual of turning my favourite ring around on the wedding finger 3 times towards my heart that goes like this...

"I wish I may, I wish I might, hope that you'll think of me tonight".

I went to reach for my bag but the hottie Ausie sweeps in first for his bag!

"Do you mind, asshole! I was just about to get my bag, jeez where's the chivalry gone these days!" I spoke. "Oh, come on...chill out sweetheart, I didn't know that was yours." He replied.

"Perhaps the pink scarf attached to it might have given it away, no!? Now, get out of my way..." I snapped back.

"Feisty little firecracker aren't ya, hard to get- I like it...So can I have your number now?!" said the hottie.

"Uuurgh...You have got to be kidding me right!" I said. Turns out good looks aren't all they're cracked up to be. "Come on babe!" he said. "Seriously man! Don't call me babe...Do one..." I said. "See you in my dreams, beautiful". Shouts the guy. What an absolute knobhead

As I was walking to get a cab, I saw him trying to get in there too, so I rushed ahead and managed to grab it first. Who did this guy think he was...Chris fucking Hemsworth or something?

The drive to the summer camp was so stunning, I couldn't help but smile as I breathed in the fresh smell of eucalyptus trees in the air.

"Ugh, you have GOT to be kidding!" I thought to myself. "Oh, hey gorgeous!" The guy said. Eugh- he made me want to vom with his cockiness. "Ugh! You! Of course, you're here." I said.

We were then greeted by this very overly enthusiastic gay Spanish camp leader, called Franco! He was awesome though, but I just wasn't in the mood. This was supposed to be my fresh start and this guy being here just put me on edge.

"Oh, Hellooooo Haley and Ben! Come right this way darlings, welcome to Camp Algarve. We are all so excited to have you both with us this summer, we are so impressed with your resumes." Franco said. He led us through the grounds of the camp. I kept rolling my eyes as Ben started to flirt some more doing a lip puckering facial gesture as Franco was walking ahead of us wiggling his cute tight butt!

"Haley, is it?" Said Ben. He put his hand out and then grabbed my fucking hand to kiss it but I smacked it away. "Don't say a fucking word..." I said.

"You have no idea how much of an asset you two will be to our team. Here we are Haley, this is your suite, please make yourself at home. Nossa casa e sua casa! And Ben, you're just opposite over here". Said Franco. "Oh come on!" I muttered. "Is there a problem sweetie?" Franco said. "No, not at all, Haley just saw a spider ...she and I are already the best of friends from the flight here." Said Ben. You see, the problem was, we were placed in opposite cabins. Fucking perfect! "Yes, yes of course, we are going to have such a great time here." I said through gritted sarcastic teeth.

I was in such a stinker, so I entered the cabin door and dumped all my luggage on the floor and then jumped onto the bed. When I finished screaming into the pillow, I realised the stunning view out of my window. I overlooked the gorgeous lake and I stopped for a moment to catch my breath and take it all in.

You know how the typical ROM coms make you feel all warm and fuzzy inside but then when it doesn't quite go that way in real life, you get so angry with the "movies" but what if it really did happen for you. What if you just held out hope that little bit longer. Hoping is dreaming, hoping is believing and dreaming is believing. Believe you can and you're halfway there. May I just add that this applies to your entire life, not just the love of another. It's your view on all the things you want to create and if you just wish upon a space station, I really feel like you can gather some hope. I shall report back later when I'm drinking wine under the stars of the Algarve sky.

Chapter 3.

FALLING FOR YOU

We were both given the day off to explore the island before meeting the kids and starting work the next day...

I put my workout shorts on over my swimsuit and stuck some music on with my headphones in and headed out. I walked out of my cabin, taking in the stunning scenery towards the beautiful lake. I stopped for a moment, took a few deep breaths and decided to have a little swim in the lake...

I was having a nice little dip when I heard someone running nearby.

"Hello!? Anyone there?" I said. "Errr, no..." a voice said from the bushes. "Mr Australia, of course! Who else would be lurking in the trees to see me in my swimsuit!". I said. "No, no, it's not like that, I swear...I was on a run and then stumbled upon you looking fine in that bathing suit and then I, ermmm I tripped over a branch and then erm..." He said. I shoved my wet towel in his face as I walked past him... "Enjoy the water creep!" I said. "Uh, man, you've still not given me your number." "It's not like we won't see each other, mate...We're stuck at this camp for two weeks, I'm sure I'll see you!" I said. "Can't wait to see you swimming in the lake" Ben said. "Yeah, sure you can't...creep". I added.

The day after, we got up super early at sunrise with the sound of Franco's personalised tune of a trumpet.

"Wakey wakey beauties! Time for a full day of action." Said Franco.

We were then finally introduced to the kids of the camp. We were brought round to their dorms to meet them. The kids were cheeky but cuts. They had trashed one of the bedrooms with all sorts, foam from pillows everywhere etc...One kid was jumping up and down on his bed saying: "Hold back or I'll use my fart as a weapon". Another kid was also jumping up and down on his bed saying: "Look at me, I'm a speed boat", doing the noises with his tongue of a speed boat like "ppppp-prrrrrrr" Oh sweet jesus, what had we let ourselves in for!

"Yes, yes you are a speed boat little Tommy and as for you mr farty pants Sam, you can get your butts in gear for the day! This is Haley and Ben, they are your performance and water sports coaches...No cheekiness ok kids! Yes, you too miss Amber!" Franco said.

Franco turned to Ben and I and said: "I want you to both work closely with each other, combine your knowledge, sit in on some of each other's sessions. Learn from each other's strengths, I think you're both going to work well together and create something beautiful for these cheeky little creatures - my god they're a handful- you see these wrinkles, jeez I need to call my Botox therapist again... Anyway...good luck my darlings...."

Franco squeezed our cheeks as he said good luck and walked off, wiggling his butt...this guy is a hoot, but man where does he get his energy from!

Ben and I looked at each other like wtf have we signed up for! And both snap into action!

The next few days were so full on but genuinely SOOO much fun, I have to admit, even with this dude in tow. These days were mainly all about introducing ourselves properly to the kids and getting started on all the acting classes, movement, water sports, guitar and singing, the kids were so cheeky but pretty cool, actually.

On the third night, we had the evening off as the kids had their sessions with some of the other coaches and it was time for us to wind down with a cheeky glass of wine in the chill out sofa area overlooking the lake...We ate dinner with Franco, his even more flamboyant partner, Michelangelo from Italy and some of the other coaches. They were hilarious and had us in stitches of laughter. It was super cool listening to all their backgrounds and stories they had to share. Ben and I kept making looks at each other and I got the vibe something was going on here with us.

Later that night, I took a moonlit walk, and I noticed Ben was already sitting down by the lake playing his guitar...He was playing such a beautiful tune and had his notebook with him for song writing. He noticed me and stopped playing..." Oh, don't stop on my behalf, it's actually kind of nice!". I said. "Miss Haley, was that a compliment? That's quite probably the nicest thing you've said to me since we've met!" Ben said. "Well, let's not get too ahead of ourselves, I said it was kind of nice, not amazing!" I said. We smiled and giggled at each other as I sat down beside him..

"So, what brings you to this camp then hey, if you don't mind me asking, of course..." Ben said

"That's ok, I don't mind. I'll try to keep it short- I needed a break... A change from the daily grind and after a traumatic experience..."

I completely got lost in his comfort and kept talking.

"I was getting up every day at the same time, I would get showered, dressed, and shoot out for work and it just all became so monotonous and boring as hell. There was no element of surprise in my life, no challenge.

Little did I know my biggest challenge was yet to come.

I figured that after what I went through, there had to be something else out there that was more fulfilling, something more than being exhausted all the time despite earning well. I was tired of being tired and it's not what life is meant to be like.

I felt like something had to feel good again!" I said.

I began to get emotional at this point but also pulled myself together to finish my story.

I continued...

"The nights were the hardest. They still are, I guess. I felt so lonely and to a certain point, I still do. It's when all the thinking happens and it's when my mind starts spiralling into what should or could have been.

It's not easy to forget being tied down to a hospital bed by 3 strong men for doing something you're not in control of. My drink was spiked, and I was in a mental health ward for days, weeks, months and I'm not even touching on the half of it. The medication I was on made me ballon out to maybe 4 times the size I am now...It look a long time to even feel ok seeing people again without feeling like the life had been sucked out of me. I didn't want to look in the mirror - I hated who this person was staring back.

I never understood how so many people could have an option on my life choices as I was growing. Like, since when did I ever suggest anyone did something about their lives? If I asked for advice, that's different but to have to explain my choices, no, thanks I'm all good here doing my thing. As time went by, I started to feel passion again and that passion for my voiceovers and acting work along with working out drove me through the days.

Working out and lifting weights gave me a power and strength I never knew was possible, for my mind and my body. I realised I was the only one who could make me feel a certain way first. I had to be strong first for me. I'm the only one I can rely on at the end of the day. The nights were just so damn long but I had to make sure I was sleeping OK after everything I went through. Sleep deprivation played a huge role and sleeping well became part of my therapy.

It took a long time to recover but I'd sit on the same train on my commute to work into London every day, just staring out of the window and I felt empty, I felt nothing, no joy, no sadness even, just empty! In the end, my passions won over the "normal" ... I always felt like I had to have it all figured out, like I was destined to be anything or anyone, but it turns out, you don't have to have it all figured out. You learn as you go, and you go with your own timeline for anything in life because we all have a different one.

Sometimes if things get too much or feel a little overwhelming, I look up and the sky and I find great comfort in the space station. I feel connected. It's freaky but also quite awesome that sometimes I'll take a deep breath if I'm having a tough day, stare up at the sky and then suddenly the space station might go by, just by pure chance and I'll feel like I can breathe again. It's quite magical really. Or cheesy, I don't know!

I also recently just came out of a tricky relationship or "thing". He was living in my head, rent free so I had to make a change and I wasn't going to allow him to be a part of my future.

I felt like I didn't really know who I was anymore, I mean, maybe I never did! But he totally sucked my personality away. I'm glad I had the chance to love and be loved or what I thought was love at least but none of it was making me happy anymore. I wanted to be happy on my own first and I finally am. Especially being here. It feels peaceful here. No social media for a start! It's quite liberating when you don't see what everyone is up to all the time.

You know when you just feel something in your bones, and you've just got to go grab it by the horns or you'll just regret the chances or risks you never took otherwise you'd spiral into a dark hole. It might sound crazy, but I felt destined for a better lifestyle, and I knew I wasn't going to get that unless I rocked life up a little!

I already feel something shifting in me and it's only been a few days here. I trained as an actress and I now I also do voice overs, singing and writing so I've already been feeling pretty inspired since I've been here...I never got the chance to do anything creative in my old job because I was so exhausted at the end of the day that there just wasn't any headspace for that - that cut me up pretty bad cause creativity lives inside of me and it's an adrenal buzz I get so when I don't feel that, I feel so lost.

I'm also a Cancerian so I'm drawn to the water too. It may seem cliche or corny, but I needed to feel the sun on my face and the wind in my hair and hear water and nature... Plus I grew up here in Portugal so it's only natural I'm gravitated here hey.

My brothers and sisters seem to have it all figured out, they've all got their other halves and kids and steady jobs. I just didn't want to be part of the herd! Yes, I want a family one day but I just don't want it all mapped out for me anymore.

Selling houses in London just wasn't my thing anymore or wasn't ever my thing and I finally felt brave enough to walk away from the steady life, the predictability, the safe income, and live life on the edge.

I think sometimes it takes a life experience to make you sink or swim. Luckily for me, I chose to swim, or I guess I was lucky enough to swim, shall we say. Some don't get so lucky..." I finally stopped talking his ear off.

We exchanged looks. "Woah, I'm so sorry, that was not short at all! I've literally just told you my life story!" I said. "No way, I really would have never got any of what you just said from that sassy chick I first met! Nah, I'm only kidding, don't be silly, it's really nice to hear about your life, thanks for sharing that with me, it's really brave of you..." He said.

I was pretty sure we were both starting to feel something for each other at this stage. Usually, I can tell but then again, I've been SO very wrong before. A look can tell a lot but then in true me fashion, I was protecting my heart, so I quickly stole the moment away and proceeded to ask him about his world..."So, what about you then? What's your story?" I asked.

Chapter 4

IT'S FINALLY HAPPENING

Ben began: "Well, my dad passed away 5 years back and for so long, I felt like I had literally no purpose in life after he left us...I was working in a record store at the time, living with some friends in a shared house but when he died, I moved back home to be with my mum as I couldn't stand the thought of her being alone...My sister was travelling in South America at the time and she came back home when we got the news but she took off again not long after the funeral. I don't think she could handle it all and for her the best thing at the time was to be away from all the sadness.

I couldn't do that to my mum, so I supported her, she supported me. We lifted each other, we laughed, we cried. We slowly became less and less sad, but I always felt like I was missing something.

About 2 years ago, my Mum took herself off on a yoga retreat in the South of France and she came back like a new woman and had also met a new man! She had waited 3 years for it to feel OK to date and I'm so pleased for her. He's not my dad obviously but he's a decent bloke.

I felt like it was then my time. I felt inspired again and seeing my mum so happy meant I didn't feel I had to worry about her anymore...I always thought it wasn't possible to live a life without him. It didn't seem right; it didn't feel fair to his memory. Dad was such an active, kind and inspiring man. I felt like I wanted to live life through his eyes and make him proud. He was a music producer, so, when I saw the ad for the camp job, I knew it was exactly what I needed as it was something he would have done, just taken himself off somewhere for a challenge. I feel connected to him here." he said.

"Woah, thank you for sharing that with me. It can't be easy, I'm so sorry to hear that" I said. "I actually just realised I've never told anyone that before." He said. We exchanged looks again and I began to see his sensitive side coming through. "So does this mean I can take you out for dinner now?" Ben asked. "Ugh, I knew you were going to ruin the moment! Cheeky!" I said as I nudged him away jokingly.

The mood was set. It was moonlight, and we began to playfight. I got closer to the water and splashed him; he splashed me back...

Eventually, after absorbing in the moment, playing, flirting etc- We were fully in the water, staring each other in the eyes when I saw the space station go by. It was so freaky but yeah so magical that it happened to go by just at that special moment. He was so impressed that I knew it was the space station! We were slowly getting closer together and then eventually started removing our clothes bit by bit, looking into each other's eyes.

We were so close to kissing but then we heard Frank calling out for the camp dog, named Sassy. We saw torches flashing and didn't want to share this moment with anyone else of course so we slowly creeped out of the water, grabbed our clothes, and sneaked off on our separate ways. We were both smiling, looking back at each other. I felt all fuzzy and warm inside...I got back to my room, leaned on the back of the door feeling so happy! This feeling was wild. I felt like I was walking on air. I got my movie moment!

The next morning at the breakfast hall, I noticed Ben in the corner, teaching one of the boys how to play guitar. Oh, my word, my heart melted as I drooled over my cornflakes. I think I was falling in love with this guy already. I dropped my bowl on the floor, and it broke- oops! Frank came up behind me and made me jump, spilling my coffee all over me- my clumsy life hey. "Seems like someone was daydreaming hey, snap out of it, sweet-cakes." Said Franco. "No, no I, I. Um" I stuttered. "Uh, huh !! See ya later sweet cheeks." Franco said. Franco knew what was going on, I just knew it.

After breakfast, it was a fun day - water sports. I was trying my best to show off my water-skiing skills to Ben. We were all jumping off the pontoon, swinging from ropes hanging from trees. It was so much fun. Honestly one of the best days of my life laughing, joking, he had moments to wink at me, tease me. It felt so incredible! The kids loved it and so did we.

We did so many more awesome activities like baseball, table tennis, took the kids out on the quad bikes, and jet skiing. All in all, an awesome day!

The next few days were just so beautiful. We were teaching our classes but also had an absolute blast and I could really feel the butterflies start to creep in. Like, especially when we got on the jet ski together. I felt my heart beating a thousand times faster and I just couldn't help smiling! He shouted back to me: "You and I are quite different, but I think I like it". His words couldn't have been truer. This was the guy who irritated the hell out of me when I first met him but now, now all I wanted was to jump his bones and get married and have his babies!

I made a fool out of myself at times with how clumsy I am but there were so many moments where I'd catch him looking at me. Like this one time- I was doing my nighttime routine with all the meds I have to take and things I have to do for all my issues, and he saw me through the mirror- I was so embarrassed but he knocked on the door and from the other side he said: "Hey, listen there's no need to be embarrassed. I have to inject myself every day and take my diabetes meds!"

"Wait, what!? You have diabetes?" I asked. "Yeah, life can be tough, hey!" He responded.

"Woah, that can be quite heavy huh!" I said. "I guess so. I think I've just always taken it as part of my life and get on with it. So please, Haley, don't be embarrassed. Sometimes, we've just got to do things we have to do to keep us going hey! Night Haley, sleep well." He said.

"Night Ben and thank you." I responded.

That same night, I heard a knock on my cabin door when I was sleeping around 10pm. It was Ben. He asked me to keep quiet and to close my eyes. He led me outside and we walked quite far.

When he said: "Ok, now open your eyes", I saw he had surprised me with a candle lit lake setting with champagne and strawberries.

"What's all this for!? I mean it's super cute and all but is this for me!?" I asked.

"Shhhhh Haley. Just take in the moment. I did this for you. You deserve to be treated, relax, sit, let's have a drink" he said.

It was honestly THE most romantic thing anyone has ever done for me. I felt like I was in a movie or something. I never in a million years that a guy would go to this much effort for me. I felt so special, like he really cared.

"So, is this how you woe all your girls" I asked.

"Haley, do you think I just have a string of girls or something!? I'm quite a decent person you know. Now, let yourself relax and enjoy the view; I did this for you because the truth is Haley..." he said.

"The truth is what!?" I asked.

"I like you" he said.

Wait. What!? He LIKES me. No guy EVER has told me they like me first. This was huge. This was everything to me. He liked me. He saw me at my worst, and he still liked me. For me. Plain ole me. I couldn't believe it.

"You like me?" I asked. I then began to flirt with him while I played with the strawberry in my mouth, and he poured the bubbles into a glass for me. I then continued to say: "You like me huh? Well, I guess you're alright yourself. What are you going to do about it?" I asked.

"Well, considering I had to blindfold you to get you to go on a date with me, I'm pretty sure I'm doing great so far!"

I then felt a bit brave and said, "Maybe you should kiss me".

"You'd love that wouldn't you Miss Haley."

The flirting was off the charts, I guess I shouldn't share everything we talked about because, well, you know!

I got up, still looking into his eyes and flirting with him and began to walk towards the edge of the lake water. It was the most stunning evening. Clear sky, hot, no wind. Light music playing in the background. It was literally perfect. When I felt like he was walking closer to me, I gave a sexy look and pulled my hair to the side to catch his attention to my neck.

When he reached me, he moved the strap down on one side of my top and moved my hair out of my face.

I then said: "Yes, I really would love that". Shit got

real guys; this was rom com movie level stuff!

I looked up to the sky and we both commented on how beautiful it was and would you believe it, the space station went by again! It was so special. I grabbed his hand and said "Omg it's the space station. Can you see it!!? If you just look here and follow where my finger is, you'll see it. He grabbed my hand and followed the line of my finger with me. We then stopped and he pulled it down slowly. It felt like the perfect moment for a kiss, and it was. It was the best kiss I've ever had in my life.

One thing led to another and well, you know... Things happened. Romantic things happened. It was like we were in slow motion. We slowly moved back to where the blankets were, and he slowly started to undress me. Me undressing him too. His body. Oh my! His body, girls!! It was insane but I also felt his heart beating and it just felt even more special. We had such passionate love making like I'd never had before. The moon light, the peaceful surroundings. Everything was just perfect. After our love making, laughing, drinking and talking all night, we fell asleep in each other's arms. I don't think I've ever fallen asleep in someone's arms before like I was truly wanted.

The next morning, I was so confused about where I was. I had a blanket on me but Ben was gone. I thought maybe he slipped out in the night regretting what we had done so I was feeling so strange. Like, did he not want to be with me after all?

Then I saw him walking towards me with coffee and

a bagel and I was like OK, wow! This guy knows the way to my heart.

"Morning gorgeous. What a night that was." he said leaning down to give me a kiss and pass me the food and coffee.

"Ben, honestly it was perfect. Thank you for an amazing night." I said.

"Benjamiiiinnnnnn!!!" we heard a loud noise. It was Franco. He was calling for Ben. It was our day off and the kids were being take out for the day by the other camp leaders so we knew we wouldn't get caught but I couldn't figure out what Franco could possibly need from Ben right then in that moment, that moment that I was technically still naked under the blankets might I add.

"BENJIIIIIII" Franco shouted.

"I had better go see what the dude wants. Get dressed, I'll see you in a while gorgeous. I've got a special day planned for us." He said, kissing me goodbye.

I lay back and looked up at the sky. Oh, what a night! This feeling was strong. It was insanely good. I got up, looked around and slipped into the lake naked to wake me up.

I then grabbed my things to go back to my cabin, smiling like crazy and feeling on cloud 9. As I was walking past the main reception, I noticed Ben talking to a girl. I brushed it off because it could have been anything and none of my business. So, I went back to my cabin to freshen up, have a shower and get ready for this surprise, exciting day he had planned for us.

Chapter 5.

IT WAS TOO GOOD TO BE TRUE

After my shower, I got dressed, not really knowing what kind of day he had planned for me, so I wore my bikini, shorts and top, trainers and a hat.

He knocked on my door and I let him in and kissed him. "I'll just be a minute, just got to grab my sunscreen." I said.

"No worries babe, you might want to bring a towel too-Franco says we have the whole day off today." He said.

"No way, that's amazing! Ok, I'm ready now, let's go! So, where are you taking me!?"

"If I told you that, it wouldn't be a surprise now would it!"

Girls, he had the most special day planned for me. We started with a drive into the town for breakfast and then we were met at the marina by a boat that took us out stand up paddle boarding and we had a blast in the sea, it was so cool. Then we stopped off at the shore on this private little beach where he had a picnic set up for me with champagne – too cute.

Once we were finished there, we hopped back on the boat and to the marina and he had booked us into a hotel for the night, so he said to go get changed. I hadn't brought anything with me but sure enough, he had arranged this absolutely stunning dress for me to wear but before we got ready, we nipped up to the private hot tub overlooking the marina. It was just utter perfection.

I felt like cinder-fucking-ella girls! This girl was finally going to the ball! Well, I say ball but it was a place with a stunning view for our special dinner.

We were laughing and joking and flirting and just having the most incredible time. I thought I had already had the best night of my life but this really did make me feel extra special. We then went out dancing in this awesome nightclub and got back to the hotel, absolutely wasted and passed out on the bed together at like 4am, fully dressed! It was perfect. He was perfect. No guy had ever gone to such lengths to make me feel special.

I had convinced myself it was impossible to find someone like him but I was wrong, or so it seemed.

We got showered, dressed and then he had arranged the car to take us back to the camp. Smiling from ear to ear, we got back and Franco had our schedules for the day all laid out.

We had such a great day with the kids, we were really getting to know them and each other. The kids were learning so much, they were really progressing. That's what it was all about hey! The love part was just a bonus.

We got back to the camp and that girl, that dam girl was still there. Who was she!? What did she want with Ben?

Franco called Ben over and said "Pamela wants to speak with you."

Pamela!!? Who the fuck is Pamela!!?

I told Ben I'd see him later but instead of going back to my cabin, I hid behind a plant pot and eavesdropped on their conversation.

"Who is she?" the woman said.

"Haley, she works here at the camp too" Ben said.

"What the fuck Ben!?" she said.

"Pamela, it's not what you think" Ben said.

Yeah Ben, what the actual fuck. It's not what she thinks, what is she meant to think. Who is she!! Their conversation carried on but I ran off crying, speculating the worst.

A while later, I was packing up my things, ready to just leave this place because I was so upset. He had a girlfriend this whole time. I can't fucking believe it. I was so angry but so upset at the same time.

Ben knocked on my door a little after.

"Go AWAY BEN. I don't want to talk to you." I shouted.

"Haley, please, open up. It's not what you think" he said.

I suddenly opened the door and said:

"It's not what I think Ben!? What the fuck do I think? Who is she?"

"She's Pamela, my ex girlfriend" Ben said.

"God, I knew I shouldn't have fallen in love with you and now I can't trust you anymore... like every single fucking guy in my whole entire life. You want to know why I never had many relationships before? It's because I was so sure that someone would fuck it up and that I never felt good enough. I never thought anyone would take a chance on me! You were meant to be different, you were meant to be my "something/someone new" my big break... Something I didn't have to work hard at, I thought it would be easy once I felt our connection but obviously, you're incapable of telling me the truth. The truth is all that matters and you couldn't even do that.... If we don't have honesty, what do we have!!!? You know, I kept telling myself not to fall for someone who lives in Australia and look, I fell right into your little love trap...

"Jeez, Haley would you ever just stop for a moment and realise you're not perfect either. Why is this all on me!? I told you she was my EX-girlfriend. Pamela just came here out of the blue and now she's done just what I thought she would, messing with your head and mine all because she's jealous and can't accept that we broke up... how is this my fault?

We're not even together anymore, why does it matter so much!? "

"Listen to me Haley" he said, grabbing my face.

"I think you're one of the bravest, smartest, most

beautiful and courageous women I've ever met, and I think I'm falling for you deep. I have never met anyone quite like you Haley. Your stupid jokes and your clumsiness and the way you smile when your day is going great. The way you place your hair when you want me to notice you. I love you. Trust me, this is real." He continued.

"You THINK you're falling for me Ben!? You don't do everything you did for and with me if you just think you're falling Ben, so which is it?"

"Haley, come on, babe".

"Tell me you don't love her and I'll stay."

Ben literally said nothing...

"What!?" he asked.

"TELL ME YOU DON'T LOVE HER AND I'LL STAY" I said.

Ben said nothing... again.

"Thought so... I'm out of here. Have a great life asshole. Thanks for wasting my time" I said.

I heard him chase after me while I walked off to the cab ride, but he was too late, I had already got in but he started running after me and then stopped.

Chapter 6.

ALL IT TOOK WAS TWO WEEKS

According to Franco, he came back to the camp moping around and bumped into him.

Franco reiterated the whole scene for me:

Franco: What's up sweet cheeks?

Ben: I fucked up man, I fucked up bad. I just stood there and froze; I didn't get to tell her I was in love with her...I'm such a dick.

Franco: Well, yeah you are sweet cheeks. Whatever it is that's happened, what are you doing here still? You want love, go get after it like in all the romantic movies... do some big gesture and she'll be unable to resist.

Ben kissed Franco on the forehead and said...

Ben: I knew I loved you Franco, you genius...I've got to get to the airport...

Franco: Hold up!!! You didn't think you were going alone did you!? I'll get the van and the kids. Grab your guitar, come on Mr Australia, let's do this! God I really must check when my next Botox session is, this is all so many emotions to deal with!".

They all pulled up to the airport and Franco said to Ben:

Franco: Go, go, take the kids with you, I'll park up. Go get her Ben!

Ben and the kids apparently came running through the airport trying to find flight info...

Eventually they spotted me getting a coffee and all the kids shout: "HALEYYYY".

I turned around and then sequence of events goes like this:

Haley: Kids! What on earth are you doing here!

Little miss Amber: Haley, we have someone here who wants to tell you something...

Kids: Yeah Haley, come on...

The kids dragged me out of the coffee shop and they led me to Ben who was standing on a bench with his guitar...

He began to sing the song he had written for me...

The kids joined in the chorus... a crowd began to form.

Franco eventually appeared and stayed at the back with some tissues sobbing and wiping his eyes going:

Franco: Oh, it's all just such a beautiful love story...

Ben: I didn't need 2 months to fall in love with you Haley, all it took was 2 weeks.

He then proceeded to sing the most beautiful song I've ever heard. Dam Him, I was absolutely sobbing my eyes out. It was just perfect. The words, the music, his voice. It. Was. Everything.

This is how the rest of our conversation went:

Haley: But you live in Australia, how is this ever going to work!

Ben: Sometimes you've just got to take a chance Haley... we'll make this work; I know we will. You're worth every mile, every bit of expense. I'll move to Portugal if I have to.

I began to run out of the airport. It was pouring down with rain but he chased after me...We stood outside in the rain, him on a trolley shouting: "Haley, if I have to shout it from the dam runway, then I will. I love you; I don't know how else to say it."

It took me a while, ladies, cause I made him sweat like he should have but eventually I gave in to his charm and we kissed in the rain, absolutely drenched. I'd always wanted to do that.

I knew you did... I Just wanted you to work for it.

And that was it. That was the moment Ben and I knew we wanted to be with each other for the rest of our lives.

What was next for us you wonder? All the things. He moved to Portugal, just like he promised.

The proposal in the snow on our 1st year anniversary in the middle of the Austrian mountains, just how I dreamt of.

Our Ocean theme wedding by the lake the year after... Just how I dreamt of.

It was pure magic.

So, girls and guys too, of course, if you ever want something or someone, don't be too afraid of letting them in just because you've been hurt in the past.

There really are some great guys out there. They might live in Australia, but they still exist.

Trust in yourself, trust in the universe and then maybe, just maybe by wishing upon a space station, you might get what you've been looking for your whole life. Love from a very pregnant with TWINS, happy Haley xx

The End

Printed in Great Britain
by Amazon